Banana Spaghetti was not the way I had imagined it.

It wasn't yellow. It was brown. It wasn't happy. It looked miserable.

It looked worse than turnips, worse than eggplant, worse than a baked fish eye.

"Maybe it's better than we think," Julian said. "When you don't like some stuff, Mom always tells you it's better than you think."

"Will she eat it?" I asked.

"She'll eat it because we made it," Julian said.

"That might not be a good enough reason," I said.

JULIAN'S WORLD

by Ann Cameron

JULIAN'S WORLD

THE STORIES HUEY TELLS

by Ann Cameron

illustrated by Roberta Smith

A STEPPING STONE BOOK™
Random House 🏠 New York

This is a work of fiction. Names, characters, places, and incidents either are the product of the author's imagination or are used fictitiously. Any resemblance to actual persons, living or dead, events, or locales is entirely coincidental.

Text copyright © 1995 by Ann Cameron
Interior illustrations copyright © 1995 by Roberta Smith
Cover illustration copyright © by Robert Papp

All rights reserved. Published in the United States by Random House Children's Books, a division of Penguin Random House LLC, New York. Originally published in hardcover by Alfred A. Knopf, an imprint of Random House Children's Books, a division of Penguin Random House LLC, New York, in 1995.

Random House and the colophon are registered trademarks and A Stepping Stone Book and the colophon are trademarks of Penguin Random House LLC.

Visit us on the Web! rhcbooks.com

Educators and librarians, for a variety of teaching tools, visit us at RHTeachersLibrarians.com

Library of Congress Cataloging-in-Publication Data is available upon request. ISBN 978-0-679-88559-7 (trade) — ISBN 978-0-525-57987-8 (lib. bdg.) — ISBN 978-0-307-56024-7 (ebook)

Printed in the United States of America
10 9 8 7 6 5 4 3 2 1

This book has been officially leveled by using the F&P Text Level Gradient™ Leveling System.

Random House Children's Books supports the First Amendment and celebrates the right to read.

CONTENTS

Blue Light,
Green Light

My brother, Julian, isn't scared of the dark. Nighttime doesn't bother him. He just gets into bed, puts a pillow over his head, and goes to sleep.

Not me. I don't like the dark, and I get scary dreams. One I dreamed lots of times, and every time I dreamed it, it got worse. Finally I told it to Julian.

"I was walking in a high place. Then all of a sudden I went over a cliff. The whole world just dissolved. I was falling straight down to the bottom of the universe. I was going to hit it and die."

"Then what?" Julian asked.

"I woke up."

"That's nothing!" Julian said. "I've had much scarier dreams than that! Once I dreamed a lion licked my face. But I wasn't even scared!"

"A lion is not like falling!" I said. He made me mad. He always acts like nothing I say is important.

"It's no use telling you anything!" I said.

I told my mom my dream—how when I was falling, it was like my stomach climbed up into my head.

She said maybe the dream wouldn't happen anymore if my body had more calcium. She said she'd fix me warm milk with honey before I went to bed.

I told my dad my dream.

"I was falling through nowhere," I said. "There wasn't one solid thing anywhere! And I just kept dropping faster and faster all the way to the bottom of the universe."

"Huey," my dad said, "the universe doesn't have a bottom. So you can't hit it. And there isn't any *nowhere!* Everyplace is *somewhere.*"

"In the dream, it's like I'm paralyzed. And it seems like I'm nowhere."

"Maybe your mattress is too soft," my dad said. "I'll put a piece of plywood under it."

And he did. But the next night, even with calcium and plywood, I was falling just the same.

"Plywood didn't fix it," I told my dad.

"I still feel like I'm falling through nowhere."

He had just come home from work. "Give me time to think," he said.

He went into the house and sat in his favorite chair. He put his elbows on his knees and his chin in his hands. He shut his eyes and pulled his hair. He sighed.

Then he opened his eyes and smiled.

"I have just what you need in the basement!" he said.

He ran down the basement stairs and came up with something in a bag.

"Come on!" he said.

We went straight upstairs to my bed. He reached into the bag like a magician.

"*This* is the answer!" he said.

He pulled out a brand-new brick.

"How is that going to help me?" I asked.

"Feel it!" Dad said.

I felt it.

"This brick," my dad said, "is solid."

He set it down in the middle of my bed.

"Now," he said, "try it."

"*Try* it?" I said.

"Yes," he said. "Lie down on it!"

"Lie *down* on it?!" I said.

"Yes!" he said.

I didn't really want to try it, but I did. I lay back. I could feel the edges of the brick against my spine. I could even feel the three round holes in the middle of it. I sat up.

"How did it feel, Huey?" my dad asked.

"Hard!" I said.

"See!" my dad said. "That's how the world really is. Hard! Full of hard stuff.

You really *can't* just fall away to nowhere. If you sleep on this nice new brick, it will tell your body that!"

"Dad," I said, "if I lie on that brick, I will never sleep again!"

My dad looked disappointed.

"Anyhow," he said, "maybe your body will remember how it felt and not forget the world is solid. Or, if you wake up, maybe just touching it will help."

He put it next to the lamp on my night table.

"What's that?" Julian asked when he saw it.

"It's a present from Dad," I said.

"Why didn't he give *me* a present?" Julian asked.

"You don't need one," I said.

When I woke up at night, I touched the brick. It made me feel better, but it didn't stop my bad dream.

Julian and I have a friend, Gloria. I was scared to tell her about my dream. I was scared she'd nothing it, like Julian. But one day when Julian wasn't around, I told her anyway.

"That's a horrible dream!" she said. She sounded like she really understood how it was. Even though she was understanding a horrible thing, her understanding made me feel good.

"Do you get scary dreams?" I asked.

"Sometimes," she said. "Real bad ones." And she told me about them.

The worst was about some bad guys

with guns trying to break down the door to her house. She and her mom and dad pushed and pushed against the door to hold the bad guys back. And then the door broke, and she and her folks started running.

But they couldn't run fast enough...

"That dream is as bad as mine!" I said.

"Yes!" Gloria said. "And when I wake up, I feel scared and kind of sick to my stomach. And I don't want to go back to sleep. I can be brave when I'm awake—but it's hard to be brave when you're asleep."

"I wish we could signal each other when we wake up at night," I said. "So we could tell each other that we are okay."

"With lights in our bedroom windows, we could do it," Gloria said. "I could see yours shining, and you could see mine."

"We should do it," I said.

So we asked our folks for permission to buy lights and hang them in our windows. Gloria's folks said she could do it if I could. My folks said I had to ask Julian.

I thought he would say no. But he didn't. He said it was a good idea.

My dad drove us to a hardware store. We bought reflector lights with strong clamps and colored reflector bulbs. Gloria bought a green bulb. Julian and I bought a blue one.

My dad let the three of us out of the truck at Gloria's house. The clamp on the light was hard to open. Gloria's mom and dad clamped it to the windowsill for her. Gloria screwed in the bulb and plugged in the light. It worked!

At our house we got our light fixed up just like Gloria's, and Gloria stayed for supper. Afterward, she went home so we could test our signals.

Julian and I went up to our room. Exactly at nine, we screwed in the bulb. Our blue light shone out. Down the street there came an answer—a green light glowing in Gloria's window.

"It works!" Julian said. "And it isn't quite so dark in here. Sometimes it gets *too* dark. That's why I sleep with a pillow over my head."

I was surprised. "I thought you *liked* the dark," I said.

"A whole lot of it is too much," Julian said.

I thought. Maybe it wasn't just me and Gloria that didn't like the dark. Maybe it scares everybody a little.

"If it gets too dark," I told him, "you can come and get in bed with me sometimes."

And now, sometimes he does.

There's one good thing about the dark.

In daylight our signals don't show up. It's the dark that makes them beautiful.

I don't have falling dreams anymore. I don't know why. Maybe the reason is the plywood. Maybe it's my brick. Maybe it's hot milk with honey. Maybe it's because I know everybody is scared sometimes.

Now when I wake up at night, there's a blue glow in our room. I know our light is shining strong to Gloria's house. I get up and go to the window. Beyond lots of dark houses I see Gloria's green light. It is steady and bright, like a beam from a lighthouse that guides ships away from danger.

I know from her house, ours is that bright too. I stand a long time at the

window looking out from our light to hers, feeling happy.

We are okay. Me, and Julian, and Gloria.

The Rule

My mom and dad have a rule. At every meal, Julian and I have to eat at least a little bit of everything on our plates.

Julian doesn't mind. My mom says that ever since he was a baby he liked to eat every single

◆17

vegetable and all kinds of strange foods.

When I was born, my mom thought that I would be like Julian. I'm not. It's because of me that they made up the rule.

Because of the rule, I have eaten a little bit of oysters and asparagus. I have eaten a little bit of eggplant and turnips.

I have eaten a piece of radish so tiny that afterward I had to use a magnifying glass to show my parents there was something missing from that radish.

Because of the radish, they added to the rule. You cannot use a magnifying glass to prove you tasted something. You have to eat more of it than that.

There is one other part to the rule. It is about restaurants. That part is:

Food in restaurants is expensive. In a restaurant, if you order something, you better eat it *all*.

One day my mom and dad decided to take me and Julian out for dinner. They invited Gloria to come too.

My mom told us to dress up for the restaurant, with dark pants and white shirts and our best Sunday shoes. Julian tried to dress to look grown up.

I was worried about the rule. I tried to dress the best way for getting hungry. I fastened the belt on my best pants very tight. I hoped that would make me hungry.

We stopped and picked up Gloria, who was all dressed up too. She had on a pink dress and new shoes with bows on them.

The name of the restaurant was King Henry's. There were lots of cars parked out front, and there was a red carpet leading inside. A man as dressed up as us opened the door and took us to a table.

Our waiter was very tall and thin. He looked like he could eat ten dinners at once and they would just disappear inside him. He probably knew the right way to wear his belt for getting hungry.

When he brought us menus, I scrinched my neck around so I could see his belt. It was very loose! I loosened mine three notches. Right away I felt hungry.

The menu was in a leather holder. It was very big, with fancy gold and black writing. I looked for words I knew. A little card was pinned right in the middle of the first page:

Special

Grilled Giant Forest Mushrooms with Fresh Trout from Cold Mountain Rivers

---

"Special" is my favorite word. I also like the words "giant," "fresh," and "rivers." The words made me very hungry. I loosened my belt one more notch.

"What's trout?" I asked my mom.

"It's a fish," she said.

"That's what I want," I said.

"Are you sure?" my dad asked. "Are you sure you don't want a hamburger?

That's what Julian's having. Or maybe you'd like the chef's salad? That's what Gloria's having."

"I'm sure," I said. "I want the Special."

"You know you'll have to eat it when it comes," my mom said.

"I will," I said.

The thin man brought Julian's hamburger, Gloria's salad, and my mom and dad's chicken. He brought me the Special.

The giant mushrooms were all around the plate, just like a forest. The trout was in the middle. He still wore his skin and his head. His mouth was open as if he was gasping for air. His eye was big and white and sad and cooked. It looked right straight at me.

"Sorry," I said. I looked away.

I looked at the giant mushrooms. Their tops were like wings. They looked like a dark forest. They were a little mushy, but

they still looked like rooms. Probably elves
had lived under them and danced around
them in the moonlight. If I ate one, I could
be eating an elf's house.

But I had to do it. "Sorry," I said.

I took my knife and fork. I cut myself
a bite. It tasted like a buttered forest. I

liked the taste. I ate all my mushrooms.

"Huey ate *all* his mushrooms!" my mom said.

"But," my dad said, "he hasn't touched his fish."

"I will," I said.

I didn't want to touch it with my finger. I touched the tail with my knife.

The eye of the fish looked at me. I stopped touching its tail.

I wondered if I was supposed to eat the eye. If I had to, I would eat the tail first. I would save the eye till last.

I could eat the fish if I didn't look at it.

But it is hard to eat your food if you don't look at it. You keep missing the plate with your fork.

There were mirrors on two sides of the

room. I could see my fork miss the plate two ways. I could see the heaps of salad left on Gloria's plate.

"Mrs. Bates," Gloria said, "do you mind if I don't eat all my salad?"

"Of course not, honey," my mom said. "You're a guest."

I turned around in my chair and looked at the back of the room. There was an aquarium! It was full of purple fish, live ones with frilly tails like ballerinas' dresses. They were watching me. It looked like they were talking to each other. They wanted to see what I would do.

"Sorry," I muttered to the purple fish. I put my fork in my lap.

"Huey," my dad said, "we're almost done."

"Sorry," I said.

"You don't have to eat the head or the tail or the skin," my mom explained. "Just break the skin open and eat the flesh."

"Flesh!" I said.

"Meat," my mom said.

"Huey—if you finish your fish, you can have ice cream," my dad promised.

I moved my legs. My fork slipped out of my lap and so did my napkin. Right away the thin man saw. He picked them up and took them away. Then he put a clean fork by my plate. He handed me a fresh napkin.

I remembered something I saw once on TV—a live heart operation. The doctors didn't look at the patient. They kept him covered up with a cloth. My mom said they did it so they could forget he was a person and cut.

I took my fresh napkin and threw it over my whole fish, all but the middle.

Julian almost choked on a piece of bread. "Huey's napkin!" he said, pointing.

"Yuck!" Gloria said. "Huey!" my dad exclaimed. "Your manners!" my mom reminded.

I didn't listen. There wasn't time.

I picked up my fork. I took a big chunk out of my fish's side, and chewed it, and swallowed it.

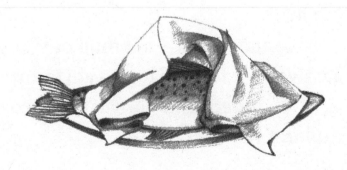

I swallowed three times extra for safety. I ate nine more big bites.

"Huey ate almost all of it," Gloria said.

"Huey has to eat it *all*," Julian said. "That's the rule!"

I looked at Mom and Dad. "Do I have to?" I said. I felt awfully full.

"Julian," my mom said, "rules aren't absolute. People make rules to make life better. If a rule doesn't work, it can be changed."

My dad said, "Huey ate a lot of good food tonight. If he eats more, he might burst."

My mom said, "I'm proud of Huey. He ate two new foods. He was adventurous."

It sounded like I was a hero. An explorer maybe.

"But what about the rule?" Julian protested.

"Maybe we don't even need it anymore," my mom said. "What do you think, Huey?"

I looked at my plate. The mushrooms were all gone. I'd eaten almost all the fish. Julian never ever ate that much. If he ever tried it in a restaurant, he could never do it.

"Let's keep the rule," I said.

Chef Huey

Food should be different from the way it is," I said to my mom. "Then I wouldn't mind eating it."

"How should it be different?" my mom asked.

"I don't exactly know," I said.

"Maybe you will figure it out and be a chef," my mom said.

"What's a chef?" I asked.

"A chef is a very good cook who some-times invents new things to eat," my mom told me.

The next day we went to the super-market. I saw pictures of chefs on some of the food packages. They were all smil-ing. I wondered if when they were little they had to eat what their parents told them to eat. Maybe that's why they became chefs—so they could invent foods that they liked to eat. Probably that's when they became happy.

The chef with the biggest smile of all was Chef Marco on the can of Chef Marco's Spaghetti.

"Please get that can," I said to my mom. "I want to take it home."

I wanted to invent something with it, but I wasn't sure what.

At first I couldn't think of anything it went with. Instead, I thought of cakes like pillows. I thought of carrots that would be fastened together around meat loaf to make skyscrapers. One night I did tie some carrots around a meat loaf my dad made— but the strings that fastened them came loose in the oven, and the skyscraper fell down.

It was the night before Mother's Day when I thought of a brand-new food.

I could see it in my mind. Something yellow. A happy yellow food. One that didn't mind being eaten.

In the morning, Julian and I were going to bring my mom breakfast in bed. Julian was going to fry eggs. I told him I had a better idea.

"What is it?" he asked.

"Banana Spaghetti," I said.

"Banana Spaghetti!" he said. "I never heard of it!"

"It's a new invention!" I said. "It will be a one hundred percent surprise."

Julian likes surprises. "So how do we make it?" he asked.

"Simple!" I said. "We have bananas and we have spaghetti. All we have to do is put them together."

Julian thought about it. "We'd better get up early tomorrow," he said. "Just in case."

At 6 A.M. we went downstairs very quietly and turned on the lights in the kitchen. We went to work.

We mashed up three ripe bananas. I took out the can of Chef Marco's Spaghetti. In the picture on the can, Chef Marco had his arms spread out wide, with a steaming platter balanced above his head on one hand.

I decided to stand that way when I brought Mom the Banana Spaghetti. I would go up the stairs ahead of Julian with her plate, so Julian couldn't take all the credit.

I held the can and Julian opened it. We put the spaghetti in a bowl. It had a lot of tomato sauce on it—the color of blood.

"We have to get the tomato off!" I said.

We put the spaghetti in the sink and washed it with hot water. It got nice and clean. We put it on a platter.

"It looks kind of spongy," Julian said.

"It will be good," I said. "We just need to put the sauce on it."

Julian dumped all the mashed banana on the top.

"Banana Spaghetti!" I said.

"Taste it!" Julian said.

But I wasn't sure I wanted to.

"You try it!" I said.

Julian tasted it. His lips puckered up. He wiped his mouth with a kitchen towel.

"It will be better when it's hot," he said.

We put it in a pan on the stove and it got hot. Very hot. The banana scorched. It smelled like burning rubber.

Julian turned off the stove. We looked into the pan.

"Not all of it burned," Julian said. "Just the bottom. We can put the rest on the plates."

We did. Then we looked at it.

Banana Spaghetti was not the way I had imagined it. It wasn't yellow. It was brown. It wasn't happy. It looked miserable.

It looked worse than turnips, worse than eggplant, worse than a baked fish eye.

"Maybe it's better than we think," Julian said. "When you don't like some stuff, Mom always tells you it's better than you think."

"Will she eat it?" I asked.

"She'll eat it because we made it," Julian said.

"That might not be a good enough reason," I said.

"You can tell her just to *try* a little bit," Julian advised.

That seemed like a good idea. "Let's take it upstairs," I said. I handed Mom's plate to him.

"No," Julian said. "You take it up. It's your invention." He handed the plate back to me.

I put the plate on a tray with a knife and a fork and a napkin. I started up the stairs. I tried holding the tray above my head on one hand, but it was very tippy. I couldn't do it the way Chef Marco did. And I wasn't happy like Chef Marco, either. I wished Julian was with me.

I climbed five steps. *It's better than you think*, I told myself.

On the sixth step I just sat down with the tray in my lap and stayed there.

I heard the door to my folks' room open. I heard feet hurrying down the stairs. My dad's.

He stopped when he saw me.

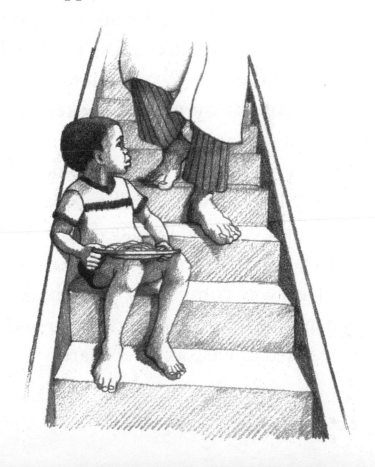

"Huey," he said, "what are you doing?"

"Thinking," I said. "What are *you* doing?"

"Going for coffee—what is that stuff you're holding?"

"It's Banana Spaghetti," I said. "I invented it. Julian and I made it for Mom. We thought it would be good. But it didn't come out the way I wanted it to."

My dad sat by me and looked at it. I passed it to him.

"It does seem to have a problem," he said. "Maybe several problems."

He sniffed it and wrinkled his nose. He got a faraway, professional look on his face, as if he was comparing it with all the banana foods he had ever tasted in his life. He looked as wise as Chef Marco.

"Banana Spaghetti," he said. "It's a good idea. You just need to make it differently."

"How?"

"Spaghetti is usually made of flour and eggs," Dad explained. "But I think we could make it from flour and banana. After I have my coffee, we can try."

We went to the kitchen. Julian had eggs out. He was getting a frying pan.

"You can put that frying pan away, Julian," my dad said. "We're making Banana Spaghetti."

He flicked the switch on the coffee maker. In a minute coffee spurted out, and he poured himself a cup and sipped it.

"I'm ready," he said. "Peel me three bananas, boys!"

We did.

"Now put them in this bowl and mash them!" he said.

We did. They came out sort of white, just like the first ones we mashed. And flour wasn't going to change the color.

"Dad," I said, "I want Banana Spaghetti to be yellow. It's not going to be yellow, is it?"

"Not without help," my dad said. "Look in the cupboard. Maybe there's some yellow food coloring in there."

We took everything out of the cupboard. Toothpicks, napkins, salt, burn ointment, cans of soup, instant coffee,

six pennies, and a spider web. At the very back I found a tiny bottle of yellow stuff. I showed it to my dad.

"That's it!" he said. "Put some in, Huey! Just a few drops."

I did.

"Stir that yellow around," he said.

We took spoons and did it.

"Bring me the flour," he said.

We did.

He dumped some in the bowl.

"This is tough to mix," my dad said, "so let me do it."

With a fork he mixed the flour and banana into a dough.

"Julian! Spread some flour on this counter!" he said.

Julian did.

My dad set the dough on the floured counter. "I have to knead this dough," he said. "You boys clean the cupboard and put everything back in it."

We did, except for the pennies. We asked if we could have them, and my dad said yes. We put them in our pockets.

Dad rolled up the sleeves of his pajamas and pushed the dough back and forth under his hands, twisting and turning and pressing it hard, until it was smooth and not sticky.

"The dough has to rest so it will be stretchy," he said. He covered it with an upside-down bowl and put a big pot of water on the stove to boil.

"What should go in the sauce?" he asked. "It's your invention, Huey, so you decide."

I tried to think of the best ingredient in the world.

"What about—whipped cream?" I asked. I never had any spaghetti that way, but I thought it would be good.

"Whipped cream! A great idea!" my dad said.

I poured cream into a bowl. Dad got the electric mixer out, and I beat the cream.

"How about—sugar?" Julian said.

"Sugar is right," I said. Julian poured some in.

"Now," my dad said, "what about spices? How about—oregano?" And he gave me the oregano bottle so I could smell it.

It smelled like pizza. "No!" I said.

"How about—cinnamon?" he asked.

Julian and I both smelled the cinnamon. "Yes!" we said.

"And how about—ginger?" He handed me the can.

Julian and I both smelled it. Julian said no. I said yes. Banana Spaghetti is mine, so I won. My dad shook in some ginger, and then he beat the cream till it was thick and fluffy.

"How about—sliced banana?" Julian asked.

I said yes. We sliced a banana. My dad stirred it into the cream.

We all tasted the sauce. It was delicious.

"Now," my dad said, "the spaghetti."

He uncovered the spaghetti dough and asked us for the rolling pin and the flour.

He rolled the dough, and then we rolled it some. Finally, when it was thin and stretched out like a blanket, he folded it over two times and cut it into strips.

Julian and I separated the strips and

unfolded them. They were long and smooth and yellow. We held them in our hands gently, like Christmas tree tinsel.

The water in the pot was boiling as if it wanted to jump out. We stood on chairs by the stove and dropped in all the spaghetti strings at once. They sunk and swam in the pot for just a minute before my dad dipped in a fork and fished one out.

He tasted it.

"Done!" he said. "Quick! Get the plates ready!"

We did. Dad set a strainer in the sink. He poured everything out of the pot. All the water washed down the drain. The spaghetti stayed in the strainer. He divided the spaghetti on the plates and shook some cinnamon over it. I spread the sauce on top. It looked good—except for one thing.

"Just a minute!" I said. I found a bag of chopped peanuts and tossed some on top of each plate of Banana Spaghetti.

"Is that everything, Huey?" my dad said.

"Yes," I said.

"Delivery time!" Julian said.

I went first with two plates. Julian came behind me with the other two plates. My dad came last, with silverware, coffee, and orange juice on a tray.

My hands were full. I knocked on the bedroom door with the edge of one plate.

"Come in!" my mom said. I hoped she would be just waking, but she was sitting up in bed, reading a book. She looked hungry.

I set one plate on the bureau. I brought the other to her the way Chef Marco would have done it, held out like a gift.

"Happy Mother's Day!" I said.

"What *is* this?" she said.

"Just—Banana Spaghetti," I said.

My dad handed her a fork. She tasted it.

"Delicious!" she said. "Very strange, but *very* delicious."

"Dad and Julian helped me," I said. "But it's my invention."

We arranged everything so we could all eat on the bed. When we had eaten all the spaghetti, we had second helpings of sauce.

My mom scooped up the last bit of her sauce with a spoon. "Banana Spaghetti! What a wonderful breakfast!" she said.

And I was very proud. Just yesterday there was no such thing as Banana Spaghetti in the whole world—and now there is. Just like one time the telephone didn't exist, or television, or space stations. A lot of people believed those things could never exist. But then some great inventor made them.

I am an inventor. And a chef.

And I know what I want for dinner on

my birthday. Banana Spaghetti. With chocolate shavings over the sauce, and seven yellow candles on the top.

Tracks

Julian had a book from the library. By reading the book, he was learning to be a tracker and a guide and a scout. He had shown it to Gloria. He wouldn't show it to me.

"I could learn too," I said.

"You couldn't!" Julian said.

"I could too!" I said.

Julian shook his head. "A tracker is strong and silent. You're too little—and you talk all the time."

I hate it when Julian acts like that. It makes me want to fight him. But I didn't say one word. I just went away.

In the night I woke up and went downstairs. Julian's book was lying on the couch in the living room. I picked it up. I couldn't read it all, but I could see it was about tracks.

It had pictures of the hoof and paw prints of almost every kind of animal. It showed deer tracks and raccoon tracks, the tracks of zebras and giraffes and elephants.

I looked out the living room window. I could hear the wind. I could almost hear many animals outside. Very quietly I opened the front door and went out. I still had the book in my hand.

There was a full moon. I could see my own shadow on the grass, but I couldn't see any night animals. I looked for tracks, but there weren't any.

In real life I really had seen raccoon tracks once. I looked through Julian's book until I found some. I decided to copy them. I found a sharp stick and went to where our driveway divides our lawn in two parts. The driveway isn't paved. It's pebbly and sandy.

Raccoon tracks look almost like human

hands, with narrow fingers and long, sharp claws for fingernails. I stood on the grass and used my stick to copy them along the edge of the driveway.

I walked on the grass to the street. Then I walked on the paved street to the other side of our driveway. I copied more rac-

coon tracks on that side—so it looked like the raccoon had turned around and gone back to the street.

I hid my drawing stick in the hedge and went back in the house. I was careful not to leave any footprints. I put Julian's book back on the couch, just the way he'd left it. I climbed the stairs, tiptoed past Mom and Dad's room, and went back to bed.

In the morning I went down to breakfast. Julian was running into the kitchen with his book in his hand.

"Dad! Dad!" he shouted. "A raccoon was here last night!"

"Really?" my dad said. He went outside with Julian to study the tracks, and I went along.

Julian showed Dad his book. When Dad bent down to look at the tracks, I tried to look at Julian's book too. But Julian wouldn't let me. Whenever I tried to, he covered it with his arm and poked me in the ribs with his elbow.

My dad stood up. "It sure does look like a raccoon was here!" he said. "Sometimes those little rascals come round to eat food out of garbage cans. From now on, we'll need to keep the lids on tight."

The next night I woke up. I looked at the clock that sits on top of the brick on my night table. It was 1 A.M.

Julian was asleep with his pillow over his head. I went down to the living room.

I found his book on top of the TV, open to a page on African safaris. I went down to the basement and got my dad's hammer. I took it and the book outside. The moon was not quite as big as the night before, but there was plenty of light for working.

Every few feet I mashed up small spots of sandy ground with the hammer. Then I rounded them out just right.

I stood up and compared them to the picture in Julian's book. They looked the way they were supposed to—just like zebra tracks. Zebras leave hoofprints like horses. Their tracks are deeper in the ground than raccoon tracks. That's why I used the hammer.

In the morning, Julian was so excited he was yelling.

"Mom and Dad!! Huey! Come look! There was a *zebra* here last night!"

We all ran outside. My dad studied Julian's book and the tracks.

"Hard to believe," my dad said,

"but it sure does look that way!"

"Could it have been a horse?" my mom asked.

"All the horses around here wear shoes," my dad said. "These tracks don't show shoe prints."

Gloria came over and saw the tracks. *"Ama-a-a-zing!"* she said.

She and Julian decided to make a zebra trap. They made the cage out of straight sticks tied together with rope. I brought them the rope from the basement.

"We should put a carrot in the cage to attract the zebra," Gloria said. So Julian did.

He asked permission to sleep on the front porch, so he could watch for the zebra and catch it. Gloria got permission to sleep over and help.

Julian asked if I wanted to sleep down-stairs with them to watch for the zebra. "We could take turns watching and sleep-ing," he said.

I said there wasn't room for three of us on the porch. Besides, I was tired.

But in the night I woke up. I looked out the bedroom window. The moon was not as big or as bright as the night before. I went to the basement and got a hammer, a chisel, and a flashlight. I crossed the liv-ing room on silent feet and peeked out the window to the porch.

Julian was on the floor in his sleeping bag with his pillow over his head. Gloria was sitting up with her back against the wall, facing the zebra cage. But her head was tipped over on her shoulder. She was asleep.

On tiptoe I went out on the porch. The porch has one board that squeaks. I didn't step on it. The tracking book just touched Julian's hand. I put the hammer, the chisel

and the flashlight under my left arm. I was scared I would drop them. I bent down. Very carefully, I reached out with my right hand. Very gently, I took the book. Julian and Gloria did not wake up.

I walked to the zebra cage. I set my tools down on the grass.

Carrots are one of my favorite foods. I picked up the carrot in the cage. I bit off half and ate it. I used the flashlight to check the rest of the carrot for tooth marks I had made on the other half. I worked on them with my fingernail to make them look bigger. Then I put the flashlight down and put the carrot back in the trap.

I used the hammer to make more zebra tracks—into the trap and back out again.

I checked them with the light from the flashlight. They were okay. When I finished, I found a fallen pine bough. I used it to brush out all my own tracks.

I went to the edge of the street. At the edge of the street there is a narrow, sandy place. There was room for some very good tracks. Elephant tracks!

Elephants are *really* heavy. Their tracks

sink in. I used the chisel to soften up the ground before I made the tracks with my hammer. I made fat, round tracks, with bumps for the toe marks—five each on the front feet and three on the back, just like the picture in Julian's book. Afterward, I shined the flashlight on them. They looked good.

"The zebra was here!" Gloria said in the morning. "He was *here*—but I fell asleep. Huey! You should have helped us watch for him!"

"I'm too little," I said. "I'm afraid of zebras."

Julian and Gloria took my mom and dad and me outside and showed us the tracks—and the marks in the carrot.

My dad studied the carrot. "Those are tooth marks all right," he said.

My mom took the carrot and examined it. "*Some* kind of tooth marks..." she said. "But—" She never finished what she was going to say, because Julian was shouting and pointing at the street.

"There're more tracks out here! HUGE ones!"

We all went running to see.

"They look big enough to be elephant tracks!" Gloria said.

My mom said, "What I don't understand is why all these animals are coming to our house. Do you have any ideas, Huey?"

Everybody looked at me. I had to say something.

"It's really strange!" I said.

I am a tracker and a scout. I am strong and I am silent. I know many things. But I keep them to myself.

My Trip to Africa

I looked up. The sky was blue, perfectly blue. I wanted to know why.

I went down to my dad's workshop in the basement. He was working on Julian's bicycle.

"Why—" I began.

"Can it wait a minute, Huey?" my dad said. "I'm trying to figure this blamed thing out."

I went upstairs to the den. My mom was sitting at the desk.

"Mom, why is the sky—" I began.

"Oh, Huey!" my mom said. "I was adding numbers in my head for income tax, and now I have to start all over again!"

I went outside. Julian and Gloria were kneeling on the lawn, working on a new, improved zebra trap.

"Julian," I said, "why—"

"Look at this!" Julian interrupted. "We have the carrot partway under a rock. A rope is partway under the rock too. When the zebra picks up the carrot, he'll move the rock and loosen the rope. That will make the cage door fall shut—and we'll catch him!"

"What if the zebra is too smart?" I asked.

"What do *you* know about zebras?" Julian asked.

"A real zebra would kick that cage to pieces!" I said.

I went back into the house and dived onto the couch. I didn't want to know about the sky anymore.

It's not blue all the time, anyhow, I thought. *Most of the time it isn't. So who cares?*

I stared at the living room wall. It had

some interesting things on it—things from Africa my mom had hung up there—a straw hat from Ghana, with green and yellow designs in it; and a cloak from Mali with bright blue and orange and white stripes; and a walking stick from we're not sure exactly where, with the head of a lion carved on it.

I kept staring at the things. The things kept staring back at me—especially the lion's head on the walking stick. Pretty soon I realized something. I wanted to go to Africa. I wanted to see where the wild zebras are. If I lived in Africa, I would be happy.

I went into the kitchen and made three peanut butter sandwiches. I put them in a plastic bag and put the plastic bag in my backpack. Then I went back into the living room. I stood on a chair and got the hat, the cloak, and the walking stick off their hooks.

I put the hat on my head. It was too big, so I put the cloak over my head first, and then the hat on top of it. That way, it fit just fine. I tried holding the walking stick. It felt just right.

I went out the door. I passed right by Julian and Gloria. They were working so hard on the trap that they didn't even see me.

I went down the street. The hat was good. It kept the sun out of my eyes. The cloak was good too. It felt warm. And the walking stick was the best of all. It seemed to want to go places without my even moving it.

Once someone had carried it all over Africa. He had leaned on it when he was tired. He had used it to cross rivers. When he needed to, he had used it as a weapon.

Right where my hand held it, it was smooth and shiny. The African hand that used to hold it had polished it for me. If I held on to it and didn't let go, it would show me the way to Africa.

I walked eight blocks. I got to the mall where the gas station is. I know the man who works at the gas station. His name is George. I asked him the way to Africa. He pointed.

"It's east of here," he said. "But be careful of the traffic."

I walked the way he pointed—toward where the sun was coming from. I used my stick to climb the hill above

the gas station. I know the man who works on people's lawns up there. His name is Oscar. He was planting tulips.

"That's a nice stick you've got. Nice hat and cape too," Oscar said.

"Thank you," I said. "Do you happen to know the way to Africa?"

Oscar pointed.

"It's west of here," he said. He was pointing me right back where I came from!

"George at the gas station just told me it's east," I said.

"You can get there going east too," Oscar agreed.

I kept going the way I had been going.

My legs were getting tired. I saw a woman sweeping her steps. I've seen her lots, but I don't know her name. She looks old and wise. She looked like she should know the way to Africa.

"It's south of here," she said. And she pointed. "South and east. Or, south and west. You could do north too—but that would mean crossing the polar icecap."

"Everybody keeps telling me a different way to Africa!" I said. "Somebody is telling me lies!"

"No," the woman said. "No, they're not. Look!" she said, and held her arms out in front of her, wide and curved.

"The world is round, like a ball," she said, "so there's more than one way to anywhere."

She drew paths in the air with her finger. She explained everything so well that I could imagine all the seas and mountains I would cross, and all the rounding I would do to get to Africa.

I thanked her.

"Good luck," she said. "The shortest way is about six thousand miles."

I turned south. My feet hurt a little, but I was happy. Because the whole world is connected. So even if it was a long way, I couldn't miss Africa. Even if I made a few mistakes, someday I would get there.

Big clouds formed in the sky. They looked like the walls and towers of the ancient palaces in Africa. They made me glad I was going there.

I got to the park where Julian and Gloria and I go sometimes. I went through the park to a big log we like to play on. I sat down.

Right in front of me was a tree. A dog

stuck his head out from behind it and looked at me.

He was little and thin, with brown eyes and a tail that curved like a question mark. He had a cut on one of his ears.

I called him.

"Here, boy!" I said.

He perked up his ears as far as they would perk, but he didn't come closer.

"I won't hurt you," I said.

He sat down. He looked like he was wondering if he should believe me.

My backpack was under my cloak. I took it off and got out my sandwiches. I held one out to the dog and said, "Food, boy!" but he still wouldn't come.

"I'll call you 'Spunky,'" I told him. "You're hungry—but you still won't come just because a stranger calls you. That's being *spunky*."

He looked like he understood.

I put the sandwich on the ground halfway between us. Spunky walked up to it. He ate it in a gulp and stood and looked at me.

I finished my own sandwich.

"Do you want to go to Africa, Spunky?" I asked.

His body looked like he was saying no. His eyes looked like yes.

"Come on, then," I said. I got up and started walking again. Spunky followed me, not too close behind.

It was beautiful and peaceful in the park. By the river, lots of yellow flowers were growing. I decided to pick some for my mother. She couldn't help it that she couldn't add when someone talked to her. Probably only a genius could do that.

Then I remembered I was going to Africa. I couldn't take her any flowers if I was going to Africa. I sat down to think. I took out my last sandwich. I ate half and threw half to Spunky. He caught it in his mouth.

"We're going to Africa," I said. "But we don't need to go right away. We can go later. When we're older. When I have hiking boots."

I picked some of the flowers for my mother. I found a special stone to show my dad and Gloria. And Julian, maybe.

"Spunky," I asked, "do you want to come with me to my house?"

Spunky cocked his head as if he was deciding something. Then he followed me.

When we got close to home, I could hear voices calling me. My mom's, my dad's, Julian's, Gloria's. In the distance I could hear Gloria's mom and dad too, calling "HUUU-EY! HUUU-EY!"

Spunky looked at me and sat down by the driveway. I walked closer to the house. My mom had her back to me. She was shading her eyes from the sun and looking into the hedge.

"Come out, Huey!" she shouted. "This is *not* a joke!" She sounded worried.

I came up behind her.

"Here I am!" I said. I handed her my flowers.

She didn't even look at them, she just held them upside down with the stems squeezed tight in her hands.

"Huey!" she said. "Where *were* you? You know you're not supposed to go anywhere unless you tell us first!"

"You were busy and Dad was busy," I said.

"We are never *that* busy!" my mom said. "We need to know where you are."

I saw my dad down the street. He saw me and waved to Gloria and her mom and dad. They all came running up, out of breath and upset-looking.

"Huey!" my dad said. "Do you know how long you were away?"

"I don't know," I said. "I was going

to Africa, but I decided I didn't need to go right now. So I'm back."

"Huey," my dad said. "You must *never* do this again. Most people are nice, but some aren't. You could be in a dangerous place and not know it. A bad person could just reach out and grab you and that could be the end of you. No trip to Africa. Not even a trip home."

"I didn't go close to anyone," I said. "If anybody had tried to grab me, I would have run and screamed."

My dad stood over me and held me by the shoulders. "Next time you *ask* before you go somewhere!" he roared.

"Yes, sir!" I said.

Spunky barked. He was watching Dad and me. He had his two front feet on our lawn and his two back feet in the street. He looked like he was worried about what Dad would do to me.

"That's Spunky," I said. "He's my friend. I met him in the park and he came back with me. I don't think he has a home."

"And you want him to live with us?" my mom said.

"Yes," I said.

Everybody looked at Spunky. "He looks to be abandoned," Gloria's dad said. "Skinny. No collar."

"Can we keep him?" Julian said.

My mom and dad looked at each other.

"We'll have to call the animal shelter first," Mom said. "We have to make sure no one lost him."

"I'll call," I said.

Julian stayed out on the lawn with Spunky, so he wouldn't go away. The rest of us went into the house and I called. Nobody had lost a dog that looked like Spunky.

"If nobody shows up to claim him, you can keep him," Dad said. "But if you *ever* go off without telling us, he's going to the animal shelter. And he won't be coming back."

"I'll remember," I said. "I won't go any-place without telling you."

So that's the way it was. We persuaded Spunky to come in the house and eat. And he stayed.

My mom put eggs in his food, and his coat got shiny. And now he trusts us. He's

my dog and Julian's and partly Gloria's
too. But mostly, he's mine. I'm the one
who found him. I'm the one who named
him.

When I feel bad, I can tell him things I
can't even tell Gloria. When I'm sad, he
puts his head on my arm and licks my
hand. He makes a little moan in his throat
and shows by his eyes that he understands.

The cloak and the hat and the walking

stick are back on the wall. I'm glad they went on a trip with me. Things like to be used.

The world is a lot, lot bigger than I ever knew. And sometimes, I know, it can be dangerous. But it's beautiful too. And someday I will go to Africa.

P. S.

Julian hadn't found any more tracks. He really, really wanted to see a zebra or an elephant. He got the idea that if we had a tree house, we could stay out of sight and watch for wild animals from above. So my dad helped us make a tree house in the pine tree in front of the house. It has a big platform, big enough for all of us—Julian and me and Gloria—to lie on. It has steps up the trunk that you can climb to get to it. And it has a special rope ladder you can climb too.

One day Julian figured out how to get Spunky up there by putting him in a basket that we hauled up with a rope and a pulley. I think Spunky liked being with us, even though he thought it was a long way off the ground.

Once we got him up in the tree house, Julian started wondering.

"Maybe it's because of Spunky that the animals don't come around anymore," he said. "Maybe they smell him and are scared of him."

I wasn't going to say anything. I am a

tracker and a traveler and a scout. I am silent. But I couldn't stand to be silent anymore.

"Julian," I said, "*I* was the raccoon. *I* was the zebra. *I* was the elephant."

And I explained it all.

Julian got very angry.

"Why did you do that to me?" he said.

"Because of the way you treat me," I said. "You treat me like I'm little and can't do anything. I decided to show what I can do."

"It was a great trick!" Gloria said. "Huey isn't a little kid. And Julian, you deserved it."

Julian still looked mad. "You aren't a little kid," Julian said. "You're smart. But don't do that to me again!"

"If you don't treat me bad, I won't trick you," I said.

Since then, Julian and I are friends. He even showed me everything in the tracking book, and read long parts to me—parts about the habits of animals, like how they like to come to water holes at dusk.

The three of us read that together, and it gave us the idea of making a water hole under the tree house. We put a big tub of water down there and a smaller, shallow one. We fill them with fresh water every afternoon. Then we go up into the tree house to watch for animals.

So far some birds have come and taken big, splashy baths in the shallow tub. Gloria's mom says if she helps out at home, Gloria can take some binoculars up to the tree house so we can see the birds even closer. My dad says he'll get us a book and an audiotape so we can identify different kinds of birds—and get them to come to us by copying their songs. He said he met a man once who had studied birds his whole life. He knew how to call hundreds of different birds that way. He would just make one or two calls, and out of nowhere, dozens of birds would come flying to him. Maybe one day we can do it.

My dad says if anybody finds wild animals around here, it'll be us.

I think he's right.

ABOUT THE AUTHOR

Ann Cameron is the bestselling author of the Julian's World series and many other popular books for children. She lives in Guatemala. Find her online at anncameronbooks.com.

Don't miss the next book about Huey!

More Stories Huey Tells

The top of the ladder looked a long way down. I thought of saying I wouldn't go down—but if I did, they'd all think I was scared.

Julian told me not to look at the bottom of the mine, just to lie on the ground and dangle my legs down toward the ladder and they'd let me down. I let myself off the edge of the mine and the rope pulled tight. I heard Spunky start whining and barking and Julian telling him to be quiet. But it was only a few seconds before I felt my feet on the ladder, and I climbed down it to the bottom of the mine.

New friends. New adventures.
Find a new series . . . just for you!

For ballerina and fairy and vampire lovers

For adventurers

For storytellers

For dog lovers

For mermaid and cat lovers

For sports fans

RHCB **RHCBooks.com**